CHEESE

From Start to Finish

by Claire Kreger

Photographs by Patrick Carney

BLACKBIRCH®
PRESS

San Diego • Detroit • New York • San Francisco • Cleveland • New Haven, Conn. • Waterville, Maine • London • Munich

For more information, contact
The Gale Group, Inc.
27500 Drake Rd.
Farmington Hills, MI 48331-3535
Or you can visit our Internet site at http://www.gale.com

Photo Credits: Cover, all photos © Patrick Carney, except page 3 © Getty Images; pages 4, 5, 7, 24-25 © Hilmar Cheese Company

LIBRARY OF CONGRESS CATALOGING-IN-PUBLICATION DATA

Kreger, Claire, 1973-
Cheese from start to finish / by Claire Kreger ; photographs by Patrick Carney.
    p. cm. — (Made in the USA series)
Summary: Explains how cheese is made at the Hilmar Cheese Company in California, from milking the cows to pasteurizing, processing, aging, and shipping the cheese.
    ISBN 1-56711-380-X (hardback : alk. paper)
1. Cheesemaking—Juvenile literature. 2. Cheesemaking—United States—Juvenile literature. [1. Cheesemaking.] I. Title. II. Series.
SF271.K66 2003
637'.3—dc21   2002151685

Contents

Acknowledgements
This book is dedicated to Chandra Howard, my partner in cheese.

Special Thanks
Thank you to Patrick Carney for getting all the right shots and to the kind people at Hilmar Cheese Company for making this book possible.

If you would like more information about the company featured in this book, visit the Hilmar Cheese Company website at www.hilmarcheese.com

Cheese is one of the most popular foods in the world. Not only is it delicious, it's also good for you! Cheese is an excellent source of protein, Vitamin D, calcium, and other essential nutrients. Cheese is eaten all by itself and also on many of our favorite foods. Americans eat more dairy products than any other type of food. The average American eats close to 30 pounds of cheese every year.

People all over the world eat cheese. It is an excellent source of calcium and other essential nutrients.

Each type of cheese has a special flavor. There are many different ways to eat cheese.

There are three main types of cheese: fresh (such as cream cheese and cottage cheese), soft (such as Brie and Mozzarella), and semi-hard or hard (such as Cheddar and Parmesan). Each kind of cheese has a special flavor. There are many ways to eat cheese. People eat cheese on sandwiches, melt it in lasagna, or eat it sliced on crackers.

Cheese Please!

California is the second largest cheese-producing state in the United States. About 1.6 billion pounds of cheese was made in California in 2001! Hilmar Cheese Company in Hilmar, California is the largest single-site cheese manufacturer in the world. Hilmar Cheese combines technology with quality to make many kinds of delicious cheeses. Hilmar Cheese produces more than 1 million pounds of cheese—Cheddar, Monterey Jack, and Colby—each day! So, how do they do it?

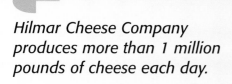

Hilmar Cheese Company produces more than 1 million pounds of cheese each day.

The Dairy

Cheese is made from milk.
Milk comes from cows.
Cows live on a dairy farm.
Most of the milk that Hilmar
Cheese Company uses
comes from Holstein
(black and white) and Jersey
(brown) cows. Dairy farms
from all over California ship
more than 9 million pounds
of milk each day to Hilmar
Cheese Company from more
than 150,000 cows!

*Jersey cows produce milk that is
very high in protein.*

Cows live in groups called herds. Herds may be small or large. When it is time for the cows to be milked, they are separated into smaller groups within the herd called strings. A herdsman walks behind the string and guides the cows to the milking parlor where they will be milked. Creatures of habit, the cows usually enter the milk parlor in the same order every day.

Most of the milk Hilmar Cheese Company uses comes from Holstein cows.

Milking the Cows

Most dairy cows are milked two or three times a day in a milk parlor. There are several styles of milk parlors. A rotary parlor looks like a carousel. It's like a merry-go-round for cows!

FUN FACT
A cow will make milk for 10 months and then rest for 2 months. Cows get a 2 month vacation every year!

Some cows are milked in a rotary parlor.

9

A milker hooks up the milking machine teat cups to the cow's udder. Teat cups use suction to get milk from the cows. In a rotary parlor, cows are milked as the parlor turns. When the cow has been completely milked, an electronic sensor signals for the cups to come off the teats. By the time a cow makes a full rotation on the carousel, she is done being milked. Each cow steps off the rotary parlor and walks back to her corral.

A milker hooks up the milking machine teat cups to a cow's udder.

Milk Receiving

Large trucks called tankers are filled with milk from the dairy farms. Drivers take the milk to a central receiving area. A milk receiver greets the driver and takes a sample of the milk.

A tanker filled with milk pulls up to the central receiving area.

11

Left: A milk receiver takes a milk sample. This sample will be tested.
Opposite: Tankers filled with milk are hooked up to hoses that carry the milk into giant silos.
Inset: A receiver hooks up the hose to the tanker.

The milk receiver lowers a small "dipper" into the tanker. This milk sample is taken inside a building to be tested to ensure the milk is of excellent quality. When the driver is given the "all clear" signal, he or she drives to where the milk is unloaded from the tanker.

A milk receiver hooks up a hose to the back of the tanker. Milk is pumped out of the tanker. It travels through pipes to huge holding tanks called mega silos. Each mega silo holds 200,000 gallons of milk! That's equivalent to 3.2 million glasses of milk! Milk is stored in the silos until it is moved along to the next stage.

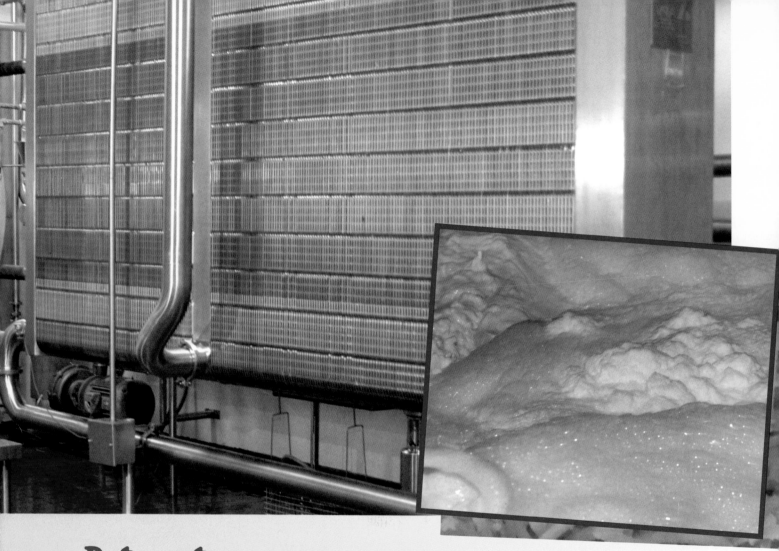

Pasteurization

The next step in cheese making requires that the milk from the silos be heated. Heating milk to kill harmful bacteria is called pasteurization. This ensures that milk is safe to be used to make cheese.

14

Left: *Milk is pasteurized in this machine to make sure it is free of harmful bacteria.* **Inset:** *Milk foams up when it is heated.*

Milk travels through pipes from the silos to a machine that heats it to 165 degrees Fahrenheit. At this high temperature, it only takes 16 seconds to kill any harmful bacteria. A plant operator monitors the computer that runs the pasteurizing equipment to be sure that the temperature stays at 165 degrees.

An operator makes sure the pasteurizing machine stays at 165 degrees.

15

Louis Pasteur: Science Pioneer

Louis Pasteur is considered the father of modern medicine. He discovered that microbes, or germs, are the cause of many diseases. He figured out how to use weakened microbes to make vaccines for diseases such as chicken pox, cholera, anthrax, and rabies. Out of this work came the science of immunology—the study of a body's defenses against germs. Even though Pasteur was the father of immunology, he is best known for his work with heat as a method to kill germs.

Louis Pasteur is the father of the study of immunology.

Pasteur figured out that microbes (germs) did not spring up in sealed containers, but that they were airborne. In the mid-1800s, wine makers in France were unable to keep their product from spoiling. They called on Pasteur to help. Pasteur realized that microbes had infected the spoiled wine. He discovered that microbes could not survive in high temperatures. Pasteur experimented with heating the wine. He found that at 122–140 degrees wine was prevented from spoiling. Pasteurization had been invented.

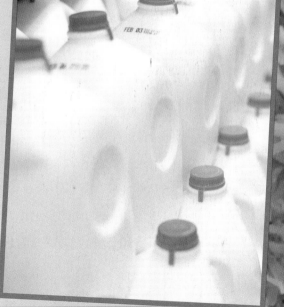

Like winemakers, dairy farmers realized that milk also carried germs that could make people sick. They began to heat milk to kill germs. They found that cooking raw milk at 165 degrees for 16 seconds was enough to kill all microbes. Today, pasteurized milk is the standard in the industry.

Pasteurizing milk is a standard practice today.

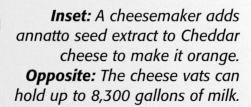

Into the Vats!

Once milk is pasteurized, it travels to a vat that can hold up to 8,300 gallons of milk. Certain ingredients are added. A starter culture—or a "good bacteria" created in a lab—gives cheese its flavor and texture. Other ingredients are automatically released through pipes into the vats. A chemical enzyme called rennet is added to thicken the milk. Calcium is also mixed in. Extract from annatto seeds is added to Cheddar cheese to make it orange.

Inset: A cheesemaker adds annatto seed extract to Cheddar cheese to make it orange.
Opposite: The cheese vats can hold up to 8,300 gallons of milk.

Blades constantly turn inside the vats to separate milk into liquids and solids.

The mixture is cooked at 96-101 degrees Fahrenheit. Blades constantly turn inside the vats. This separates the milk into solids and liquids called curds and whey. The solids are the curds. The liquids are the whey. The curds are now considered cheese.

The Cheese Belt

After leaving the vats, the curds move along a cheese belt. At this point, the cheese is still "soupy." Large rakes, called agitators, stir the curds to keep them from sticking together as the remaining whey is removed for processing.

As the cheese is carried to the next stage on the belt, other ingredients are mixed in. Salt is added to all cheese for flavor. Special ingredients, like peppers, garlic, or pesto may also be added at this stage.

Cheese moves along a cheese belt. Special ingredients are added to certain cheeses for flavoring.

Whey Protein and Lactose

The liquid (whey) is separated from the curds and sent to other facilities to be processed and dried. Whey contains protein, lactose (a natural sweetener), and water.

Whey is sent to the on-site protein and lactose plants to be processed.

Protein and lactose are separated and sent through huge stainless steel dryers. When protein and lactose are dried, they form a powder. Hilmar Cheese packages and distributes whey protein and lactose all over the world. Whey protein and lactose are used as ingredients in a wide variety of food and nutritional products, such as sports drinks, baked goods, infant formulas, and even candy!

Lactose powder is packaged and shipped all over the world.

Hilmar History

In 1984, twelve dairymen founded Hilmar Cheese Company. The dairymen wanted to make cheese from their all-Jersey herds, which were known for producing high-protein milk—ideal for making cheese.

  In 1985, Hilmar Cheese Company opened its cheese plant and began producing American-style cheese. At the time, the company made only 3 vats of cheese per day with milk shipped from only 15 dairy farms. The company grew very quickly, though, and by 1987, Hilmar Cheese was making 18 vats of cheese per day.

  During the 1990s, Hilmar Cheese Company expanded its facilities to include a second cheesemaking plant

The Visitor Center opened in 1998.

to accommodate the company's growing cheese production. In the mid–1990s, California became the nation's top milk-producing state—and Hilmar Cheese Company was making up to 550,000 pounds of cheese per day. By 1996, the company was the largest single-site cheese producer in the world. By 2002, the company's daily production exceeded 1 million pounds.

Hilmar Cheese Company founders. **Front, seated:** Donald Sherman and Lloyd Nyman; **Middle, seated:** William Ahlem, Sharon Clauss, Verna Van Till, Nadine Fanelli, Carolyn Ahlem, Druann Ahlem, Carol Ahlem; **Back, standing:** Vern Wickstrom, Mary Wickstrom, Ralph Ahlem, Jim Van Till, Kathy Nyman, Delton Nyman, Elsa Sherman, Richard Clauss, Dianne Ahlem, Phil Fanelli, Charles Ahlem, and James Ahlem. **Not pictured:** Paul and Dulcie Dias

FUN FACT

The room that houses the cheese towers is kept at 80 degrees.

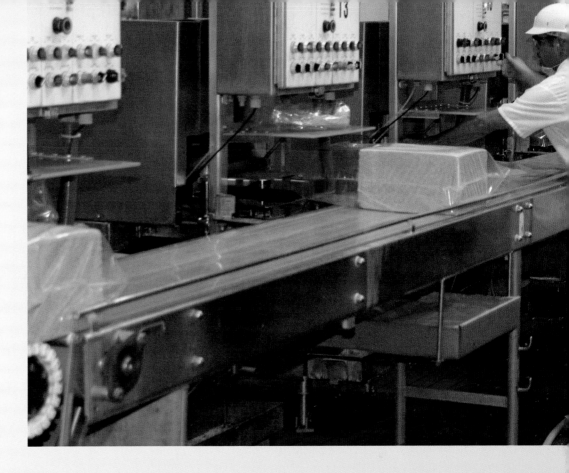

To the Cheese Towers!

Still soft, curds are moved along on the belt to the cheese towers. Cheese towers form the curds into blocks or barrels of cheese. As the cheese comes down the tower, it is sliced to fit into block or barrel forms. The cheese is then vacuum sealed inside a plastic bag and packaged into storage containers. The cheese then travels to the cold-storage warehouse before shipping.

The Cheese Lab

Samples of cheese are sent to the cheese lab for final product testing. In the lab, technicians test the cheese for pH, fat, and salt content. They also test to see how much water is still in the cheese. Technicians measure moisture levels by weighing a bit of shredded cheese. Then they bake the cheese in an oven at 100 degrees. They weigh it again. The difference in weight before and after baking determines the moisture level. Following stringent quality tests, the cheese is ready for shipment.

Opposite: A technician takes a sample of cheese to test moisture levels.
Inset: Shredded cheese ready to be tested
Right: Salt content is measured with a special machine.

Chill and Ship

Barrels and boxes of cheese are sent to a cold storage area. It is a chilly 34-36 degrees in this room! It's not long before the barrels and boxes of cheese are loaded onto trucks so this tasty cargo can be shipped all over the country!

FUN FACT

Hilmar Cheese produces 40 lb, 500 lb, and 640 lb blocks of cheese.

Left: A 640 lb block of cheese is sealed and ready for cold storage.
Opposite: Boxes and barrels of cheese are ready for shipment. *Inset:* 500 lb barrels of cheese are loaded onto a truck to be shipped.

Glossary

Agitator Large rakes that stir the curds and whey

Cheese tower Machine that forms and cuts the curds into block or barrel shapes

Curds The solids that become cheese

Dairy farm A place where cows are raised and milked

Extract Liquid in the center of a seed

Herd A group of cows

Lactose The natural sweetener present in milk

Mega silo Large holding tanks for milk at the plant

Milking parlor The place where cows are milked

Pasteurize To heat milk to kill harmful bacteria

Rennet A chemical enzyme that thickens the milk

Rotary parlor A carousel-like platform used by dairy farms as part of the cow-milking process

Starter culture Good bacteria created in a lab that gives cheese its flavor and texture

Whey The liquid that is processed into protein and lactose

For More Information

Books
Peterson, Cris. *Extra Cheese Please! Mozzarella's Journey from Cow to Pizza.* Boyd Mills Press, 1994.

Website
Hilmar Cheese Company www.hilmarcheese.com

Index